Bedtime
for
MONSTERS

Ed Vere

SCHOLASTIC INC.

For
Rufus and Phoebe

Originally published in the United Kingdom in 2011 by the Penguin Group

No part of this publication may be reproduced, stored in a retrieval system, or transmitted
in any form or by any means, electronic, mechanical, photocopying, recording, or otherwise,
without written permission of the publisher. For information regarding permission,
write to Henry Holt and Company, LLC, 175 Fifth Avenue, New York, NY 10010.

ISBN 978-0-545-91496-3

12 11 10 9 8 7 6 5 4 3 2 1   15 16 17 18 19 20/0

Printed in the U.S.A.   08

This edition first printing, September 2015

Do YOU ever
WONDER
if somewhere,
not too far away,
there might be . . .

MONSTERS?

Because supposing there
are monsters . . .

. . . do you think that

this **MONSTER**

might be licking his lips

AND

thinking about

YOU?

And if this monster *is* thinking about you,

maybe

he's thinking about you in an

EATING-YOU-UP

kind of way?

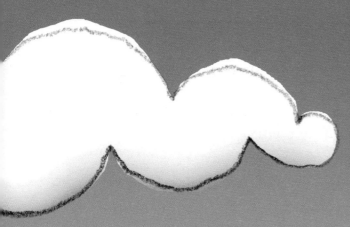

I hope not.

Because

he's coming to find you—

RIGHT NOW!

And as he bicycles bumpily
through a
dark and terrible forest

BUMP BUMPITY BUMP

do you think
he's **smiling** because
he remembered to pack
his **knife** and **fork?**

And as he crosses
the gloopy, schloopy swamp

GLOOP GLOOP SCHLOOP

do you think

he's imagining just

HOW GOOD

you'll taste

all covered in ketchup?

And as he tiptoes
through thorns and thistles

SCRITCH SCRATCH OUCH!

do you think he'll decide

you'll taste *even* more **delicious**
squished and then **squashed** onto

HOT BUTTERED TOAST?

And at this very moment,
as he climbs up the cold and snowy mountains,
getting *closer*
and **closer**
to **you**,
don't you think
he'll be feeling

VERY
HUNGRY
INDEED?

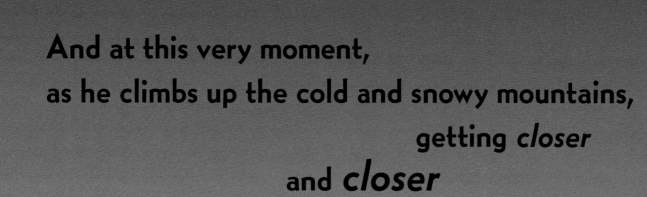

You're not **SCARED**, are you?

Because if he *is* feeling
very hungry indeed
while he searches high and low
and up and down
and in and out
all over town . . .

maybe you'll hear his **BIG** empty tummy

RRRRUUUUMMMMMBLING
and
GGRRRRRUUUUMMMMMBLING.

And if you
do hear a

RRRRUUUUMMMMMBLING

and a

GGRRRRRUUUUMMMMMBLING,

might you *also* hear a

CREAK **CREAK** **CREAK**

as he starts to climb the stairs?

And as he opens your bedroom door,

DO YOU THINK
he's **licking his lips**
because he wants to

GOBBLE YOU UP?

OH NO,

it's MUCH worse than that!

THIS monster wants . . .

a disgustingly
sloppy

GOODNIGHT KISS!

KISSY

KISSY

KISSY

Because it's

BEDTIME FOR **MONSTERS**
everywhere.

BIG ones like him . . .

and little **ones,**
just like **you.**

Did you *really* think he'd eat you up?

HOW SILLY!

Although

you *could* leave out

a little bedtime snack . . .

just in case.